Count with Me in Menominee

Read with Me in Menominee Series

S. VERNA FOWLER ACADEMIC LIBRARY

Illustrated by Janice Rabideaux

Archway Publishing books may be ordered through booksellers or by contacting:

Archway Publishing
1663 Liberty Drive
Bloomington, IN 47403
www.archwaypublishing.com
844-669-3957

Interior Image Credit: Janice Rabideaux

ISBN: 978-1-6657-3372-4 (sc)
ISBN: 978-1-6657-3373-1 (e)

Print information available on the last page.

Archway Publishing rev. date: 10/16/2023

This book is made possible by a grant from the Institute of Museum and Library Services.

Read with me in Menominee series

This book is dedicated to the memory of Maria Escalante, founding Director of the S. Verna Fowler Academic Library/Menominee Public Library. Her life's mission was to inspire children with a passion for lifelong learning and an appreciation for Menominee culture and history.

The book is set up to be read in Menominee. To assist with pronunciation a pronunciation key is included at the beginning of the book. To help you read page by page phonetics are below each Menominee word along with an image to serve as an English translation. At the end of the book is a glossary with Menominee words, the image used for the English meaning, English, and phonetics. Using the glossary with the image and English will help you learn the Menominee word as well as how to say the words.

To support you as you read to your child, a video with a Menominee speaker will be available on the College of Menominee Nation's S. Verna Fowler Academic Library/ Menominee Public Library YouTube channel. Search for "Menominee Readers." A short video will be available for each book in the "Read with me in Menominee series."

Pronunciation Key

Taken from <u>Oskēh-Wāēpeqtah Omāēqnomenēweqnaesen Wēhcekanan</u>

<u>A beginner's dictionary of Menominee</u>

Menominee Alphabet
This dictionary uses the spelling system approved by the Menominee tribal legislature. The letters of the Menominee alphabet are listed immediately below, and then are discussed in detail after that.

A ā c ae āē e ē h i ī k m n o ō p q s t u ū w y

Consonants
Most of the consonants sound like they do in English, except:
- Two of the Menominee consonants, *c* and *s*, vary more than they do in English. The *c* usually sounds like the first and last sounds in the word *church*, but for some speaker it can sound more like a *t* and an *s* together, as in *its*. The *s* in Menominee usually sounds like an English *s*, but sometimes sounds more like the first sound in the word *short*.
- *The glottal stop q is like the sound in the middle of uh-oh.*

SYMBOL	SOUNDS LIKE	FOUND IN MENOMINEE WORD
C	<u>ch</u>ur<u>ch</u>, it<u>s</u>	cīs, kanapac
H	<u>h</u>ow	tāēhkīk, pemēnesehāēw
K	s<u>k</u>ip	kōhkōpan
M	<u>m</u>at	mēnan
N	<u>n</u>ot	panāēnas
P	s<u>p</u>ot	pakāhcekan
Q	<u>uh-oh</u>	mēqsemen, pākaqāhkwan
S	<u>s</u>a<u>ss</u>y, <u>sh</u>ort	sōmen, āēmeskuahsaeh
T	s<u>t</u>op	tamāētohs
W	<u>w</u>e	wāwan
Y	<u>y</u>ou	āyosawāhkwat

Long Vowels

Menominee makes a distinction between long and short vowels. If you've ever studied Spanish, Italian, or Japanese, you'll probably notice that the long vowels ā, ē, ī, ō, ū in Menominee sound a lot like the vowels in those languages. In addition to those five, Menominee also has a long āē, and two long diphthongs, *ia* and *ua*.

SYMBOL	SOUNDS LIKE	FOUND IN MENOMINEE WORD
Ā	f**a**ther, s**o**d	net**ā**n, **ā**mōw
āē	h**a**t, s**a**t	ap**āē**hsos, an**āē**m
Ē	b**ai**t, s**ay**	m**ē**qsemen, nen**ē**kehekok
Ī	b**ee**t, s**ee**	kahk**ī**kok, nān**ī**saeh
Ō	b**oa**t, s**o**	maehk**ō**n, k**ō**hk**ō**s
Ū	b**oa**t, s**ue**	ken**ū**pik, mask**ū**cīhsak
Ia	Mar**ia**	m**ia**nīwak, p**ia**kemenan
Ua	Kahl**ua**	m**ua**kok

Short Vowels

The short vowels are all shorter in length that the long vowels are, and their pronunciation varies more than the pronunciation of the long vowels does. When they're not stressed or accented, the often sound like:

- The sound in the word *sofa* (which is called a 'schwa')
- The *i* in the word *bit*, or
- The *e* in the word *bet*.

Many of the short vowels end up sounding a lot alike, in fact. In the list below, the English words show the many different ways each short vowel and short diphthong can be pronounced.

SYMBOL	SOUNDS LIKE	FOUND IN MENOMINEE WORD
A	b**u**t, s**o**fa, f**a**ther	kōhkōhs**a**k, pak**ā**hcek**a**n, sōmen**a**poh
Ae	b**i**t, b**e**t, b**a**t	asāqcek**ae**w, maehkāēnāhkok, mīhekan**ae**h**ka**ew
E	b**i**t, b**e**t, b**ee**t, s**o**fa	māhkes**e**n, nen**e**keh**e**kok, kan**e**w, āēhsepanak
I	b**i**t, b**ee**t	ken**ū**pik, onāwan**i**kok
O	p**u**t, s**o**fa, b**oa**t	apāēhs**o**s**o**k, **o**māhkahk**o**wak, **o**qsāsk**o**k
U	p**u**t	
ya	**y**uck	ohpāē**ya**k
wa	**wo**n	mīc**wa**h, pākaqāhk**wa**n

3

Nekot (one)   otaeqciah (crane)
Nee-koot   o-taah-chee-uh

Nīs (two)   **Otaēqciahkōhsak (cranes)**
Niece   **o-taah-chee-uh-koh-suk**

Nekot (one)   awaēhsaeh (bear)
Nee-koot   Ah-waah-sah

Naeqnew (three)   **Awaēhsēhsak (bears)**
Net-new   **Ah-waah-say-suk**

Nekot (one)   **ketaemīw (porcupine)**
Nee-koot   **Kee-taam-ee-w**

Nīw (four)   **Ketaēmīkōhsak (porcupines)**
Nee-u   **Kee-taam-ee-koh-suk**

Nekot (one) mahwaēw (wolf)
Nee-koot Muh-waaw

Nianan (five) Mahwaēhsēhsak (wolves)
Nee-uh-ninn Muh-waah-say-suk

Nekot (one) **Aēhsepan (racoon)**
Nee-koot **Aah-shi-pun**

Nekūtuasetah (six) **Aēhsepanōhsak (racoons)**
Nee-koo-too-uh-suh-tah Aah-shi-pun-no-suk

Nekot (one)
Nee-koot

Nōhekan (seven)
No-hee-kun

namaeh (beaver)
Nuh-maah

Namaēhkōhsak (beavers)
Nuh-maah-ko-suk

Nekot (one)   **maehkāk (goose)**
Nee-koot   **Maeh-kawk**

Suasek (eight) **Maehkākōhsak (geese)**
Soo-ah-sick   **Maeh-kawk-oh-suk**

Nekot (one) wāpos (rabbit)
Nee-koot Waah-pus

Sākāēw (nine) **Wāposōhsak (rabbits)**
Sah-cow **Waah-puh-so-suk**

Nekot (one)   maehkaenāh (turtle)
Nee-koot   Mah-kaah-nah

Metātah (ten)   **Maehkaenāhkōhsak (turtles)**
Mih-tah-ta   **Muh-kaan-nah-koh-suk**

Nekot (one)   **mesēqnaew (turkey)**
Nee-Koot   **Muh-sayt-now**

metātah nekot-enēh (eleven)
Mih-tah-ta Nee-kot uh-nay

Mesēqnaehsēhsak (turkeys)
Muh-sayt-na-say-suk

<u>Glossary</u>

Numbers
Nekot (nee-koot) *one*

Nīs (niece) *two*

Naeqnew (net-new) *three*

Nīw (nee-u) *four*

Nianan (nee-uh-ninn) *five*

Nekūtuasetah (nee-koo-too-uh-suh-tah) *six*

Nōhekan (no-hee-kun) *seven*

Suasek (soo-ah-sick) *eight*

Sākāēw (sah-cow) *nine*

Metātah (mih-tah-ta) *ten*

Metātah nekot-enēh (mih-tah-ta nee-kot uh-nay) *eleven*

Animals
Aēhsepan (aah-shi-pun) *raccoon*

Aēhsepanōhsak (aah-shi-pun-no-suk) *raccoons*

Awaēhsaeh (ah-waah-sah) *bear*

Awaēhsēhsak (ah-waah-say-suk) *bears*

24

Mahwaēw (muh-waaw) *wolf*

Mahwaēhsēhsak (muh-waah-say-suk) *wolves*

Otaeqciah (o-taah-chee-uh) *crane*

Otaēqciahkōhsak (o-taah-chee-uh-koh-suk) *cranes*

Ketaemīw (kee-taam-ee-w) *porcupine*

Ketaēmīkōhsak (kee-taam-ee-koh-suk) *porcupines*

Namaeh (nuh-maah) *beaver*

Namaēhkōhsak (nuh-maah-ko-suk) *beavers*

Maehkāk (maeh-kawk) *goose*

Maehkākōhsak (maeh-kawk-oh-suk) *geese*

Wāpos (waah-pus) *rabbit*

Wāposōhsak (waah-puh-so-suk) *rabbits*

Maehkaenāh (mah-kaah-nah) *turtle*

Maehkaenāhkōhsak (muh-kaan-nah-koh-suk) *turtles*

Mesēqnaew (muh-sayt-now) *turkey*

Mesēqnaehsēhsak (muh-sayt-na-say-suk) *turkeys*

Printed in the United States
by Baker & Taylor Publisher Services